Dream Dogs

POPPY

D0169432

With special thanks to Lucy Courtenay and Nellie Ryan

First published in Great Britain by HarperCollins *Children's Books* 2010
HarperCollins Children's Books is a division of HarperCollins*Publishers* Ltd,
77-85 Fulham Palace Road, Hammersmith, London W6 8JB

The HarperCollins *Children's Books* website address is
www.harpercollins.co.uk

2

Dream Dogs : Poppy
Text copyright © HarperCollins 2010
Illustrations copyright © Nellie Ryan 2010

The author asserts the moral right to be identified as the author of this work.

ISBN-13 978 0 00 732039 4

Conditions of Sale
This book is sold subject to the condition that it shall not, by way of trade
or otherwise, be lent, re-sold, hired out or otherwise circulated without the
publisher's prior written consent in any form of binding or cover other than
that in which it is published and without a similar condition including this
condition being imposed on the subsequent purchaser.

Mixed Sources
Product group from well-managed
forests and other controlled sources
www.fsc.org Cert no. SW-COC-001806
© 1996 Forest Stewardship Council

FSC is a non-profit international organisation established to promote the
responsible management of the world's forests. Products carrying the FSC
label are independently certified to assure consumers that they come
from forests that are managed to meet the social, economic and
ecological needs of present and future generations.

Find out more about HarperCollins and the environment at
www.harpercollins.co.uk/green

Dream Dogs
1 - 4

Rescue Princesses
4, 5, 10 have 11

Dream Dogs

POPPY

 Aimee Harper

HarperCollins *Children's Books*

Special thanks to

The Happy Dog Grooming Parlour, Farnham

Introducing...

Name: Poppy

Breed: Yorkshire terrier

Age: 4

Colour: Caramel brown and soft grey

Likes: Dressing up

Dislikes: Plugholes

Most likely to be mistaken for: A fairy

Least likely to be mistaken for: A thief

One

Down the Plughole

It was Saturday morning. As usual, Dream Dogs was busy. Bella sat in the window, cuddling her dog, Pepper, and watching as her mum waved goodbye to Miss Waldicott and her little West Highland terrier, Angus.

"Same time next week, Suzi?" said Miss

Dream Dogs

Waldicott. "Come along, Angus. Walkies!"

The freshly washed little Westie barked and

jumped up at the treat Miss Waldicott was

holding out. The salon door clanged shut.

Suzi wiped her hands on her pink Dream Dogs overall. "My back is killing me," she sighed. "Angus is really too small for me to wash in our bath."

Bella gazed at the salon's bath. It had been built on a special platform, so that her mum didn't have to bend down too much when she was washing the dogs. But when the dogs were small like Angus, it was a bit of a problem.

"You should wash him in the sink, maybe?" Bella suggested.

They used the salon sink sometimes, for the really little dogs.

Suzi shook her head. "He's too big for that," she said. "Typical, isn't it? Most of my clients

9

seem to be small dogs. And a special small dog-bath costs a fortune."

"Three thousand pounds," Bella said, remembering her mum complaining about the cost of a small dog-bath when they had first come to Sandmouth to set up Dream Dogs. That seemed ages ago. They loved Sandmouth now, with its long sandy beach and Cliffside Primary and all of Bella and her little brother Louie's friends nearby. It was weird to think that they had once lived in London.

"Luckily they've come down in price a bit since I last looked," said Suzi. She rang up the till and put in the twenty-pound note that Miss Waldicott had given her. "But they are still

nearly a thousand pounds each. I can't possibly

afford that."

Bella checked out of the window. The pink

Dream Dogs van and mobile dog-wash trailer

was parked outside. She looked at the dark

pink lettering underneath the Dream Dogs logo

on the side of the trailer.

Paws 'n' Purrs. The Pet Shop for All Your Pet's Needs.

"Maybe you could ask the pet shop to sponsor you again," Bella suggested. "Like they did with the trailer."

Suzi shook her head gloomily. "They wouldn't sponsor me for a bath as well," she said. "No, Bella. It looks like I'll just have to put up with what we've got."

The salon door tinkled. Bella brightened. It was her favourite clients, Mimi Taylor and her little Pomeranian, Crystal.

"Morning, Mimi," said Suzi, smiling.

Mimi put Crystal down on the salon floor. The little Pomeranian perked up her fluffy

brown ears. She sniffed at Pepper in a friendly

way, before scampering up and down sniffing at

all the corners.

"You're letting Crystal run about more, I

see," said Suzi.

"She hates it if I hold her for too long," Mimi

said fondly. "I must have been crazy, the way I

used to carry her everywhere. She runs us all ragged these days!"

Crystal gave a high-pitched bark and kicked out her back legs. For such a little dog, she was a feisty thing.

"Come along, Crystal," said Suzi. "Bath time. You are one dog that fits in my sink, at any rate!"

Mimi settled on the window seat. Suzi put Crystal in the sink and started running the water while Bella fetched down a bottle of shampoo from the shelf.

"We've had a week of it," Mimi sighed. "The newspapers have been all over Idaho since he twisted his knee. Would he still play for

Sandmouth in the
new season? Is his
career over?
Honestly, it's only
a little sprain."

Mimi's husband,
Idaho Taylor, was
a well-known
footballer. When
Mimi and Idaho
had first come to Sandmouth, the papers had
gone mad. They still regularly ran stories about
them on the front page. Louie played with their
son, Pan, sometimes, as they were in the same
class at school.

"I expect it stops him from doing the

housework though, hmm?" Suzi joked.

"How did you guess?" Mimi laughed.

Bella stroked Crystal's foxy little head as

Suzi carefully soaped her body. Her creamy

butterscotch fur looked totally different when it

was wet. Usually, it was thick and fluffy but

now it was all long and straggly, dripping with water. Pepper huffed crossly from his basket. He got very jealous when Bella fussed over the dogs that came to the salon.

"Where's Louie?" Mimi asked. "Pan's been asking if he can come over to play during the holidays."

"He's with his friend Jamie this morning," said Suzi, looking round over her shoulder at Mimi. "Honestly, those two are as thick as thieves."

While the two mums chatted about the boys, Bella reached across the sink to get the washcloth her mum always used to wipe the soap off the dogs before rinsing them. Her elbow jogged the plug chain. Water started draining away. Crystal yelped and sat down very suddenly.

"Oops," Bella said. She grabbed the plug to put it back in again.

Crystal was struggling to stand up. She sat in the water as it swirled around her, lifting her paws and whining. Bella suddenly saw the problem. The suck of the plug had pulled some of Crystal's fur down the plughole. And now it was all tangled up!

"Is everything all right?" Mimi asked from the window seat.

"Bella?" said Suzi, turning back. "What happened?"

Bella tried tugging at Crystal's fur without hurting the little dog. "Nothing," she said nervously. She shielded the sink from her mum and Mimi, trying to get Crystal's fur out of the plughole as quickly as she could. Crystal wriggled and whined. "Everything's fine. The plug just slipped out. I'll have it back in a minute..."

The water stopped gurgling. Now it was a bit easier to reach down into the plughole and untangle Crystal's fur. It took a couple of goes, but she did it at last. Feeling relieved, she ran some fresh water into the sink so her mum could rinse Crystal properly.

Phew!

Her mum was right. They really *did* need a little-dog bath. But how were they going to afford one, if it cost a thousand pounds?

Two

Picture Perfect

"Thank goodness you untangled Crystal's fur!" gasped Suzi as Mimi and the freshly washed and dried Crystal left the salon with the usual tinkle of the doorbell. "Mimi would have had a fit if we'd had to cut it!"

Bella blushed. She thought her mum hadn't

seen. "It was an accident," she said.

Suzi sighed. "I know," she said. "I've done it myself once or twice."

Bella started giggling. It had been pretty funny, when you thought about it. Suzi joined in, laughing and shaking her head at the same time.

"Oh, Bella," she said. "Why is a proper small dog-bath so expensive? We'll have to think of a way to make more money for the salon if we're ever going to buy one."

The phone rang. Bella answered it.

"Mum?" she said, covering the receiver. "It's Jamie's dad. He wants to know if we can pick Louie up at the Dolphins in town in half an hour?"

Suzi checked her watch. "That's fine," she said. "My next appointment isn't until two o'clock. Come on. We can get a bite to eat down there. It's lunchtime, and I'm starving."

Pepper barked in excitement as Bella took down his lead. Suzi shut up the salon. They walked together along the seafront, towards the town and the Dolphins shopping centre.

Bella liked the Dolphins. It had only been built two years ago, and was full of brightly lit shops and colourful window displays. There were cafés, a bookshop, a shoeshop, several homeware shops and the town's pet shop, Paws 'n' Purrs. It was spread out over two floors, with a big glass ceiling that let in lots of light.

Louie was at the burger bar on the first floor with Jamie and Jamie's dad. They were all still eating their lunch, so Suzi went up and ordered some food as well. Bella sat down with Pepper at her feet and waited. Her tummy was rumbling. She eyed her little brother's chips.

"Can I have one of your chips?" she said hopefully.

"No!" Louie said. It came out as "Moof!"

"Sorry, Louie, can't hear you," Bella said,

and pinched a chip.

Suzi put a burger, chips and a bag of carrot

sticks down in front of Bella. "It's quiet in here

today," she said, looking around.

"There's something going on down at the far end of the shopping centre," Jamie's dad explained. He had a blob of ketchup on his chin. Bella looked away, trying not to giggle. "Photographs or something."

Bella craned her neck, wondering if maybe they were filming something interesting. But she couldn't see round the corner.

"Hey," she said indignantly as she looked back at her plate. "My chips!"

"Sorry, Bella," Louie giggled, munching madly. "I can't hear you!"

After lunch they said goodbye to Jamie and his

dad. As there was still a bit of time left before Suzi had to get back to Dream Dogs, Bella persuaded her mum to take them down to the far end of the Dolphins, to see what was going on.

A group of people were standing around, watching a photographer snapping pictures of a girl in a long yellow satin dress.

"Lovely! Smile a bit more, Princess!" called the photographer. "That's great – just great..."

Bella stared. The girl was standing in front of a backcloth painted with a castle. On her red-gold hair was a tall pointed hat with a floaty veil down the back. Above her head hung a sign that said: *Princess for a Day.*

"It's Amber!" Bella gasped, recognising her best friend. "Hey, Amber! What are you doing?"

Amber looked round. Her face lit up. "Hi, Bella!" she giggled. "I'm *Princess* Amber today. Mum's giving me a photo. Isn't it great?"

"You can be a princess with your friend if you want, love," said the photographer, smelling a sale. "There's a pink dress, a blue one – all sorts to choose from. You can pop them on in the booth, if your mum says you can. Only four pounds ninety-nine!"

Bella stared at the rack of princess clothes. "Can I, Mum?" she said eagerly.

"Go on then," Suzi sighed, breaking off her

conversation with Amber's mum, Claire.

Louie looked horrified and muttered something about girly dressing-up. Bella could tell that he wished he was still playing with Jamie. Ignoring him, she snatched up the pink dress and rushed into the booth. She put it on. It felt wonderfully silky and heavy. She stared at the selection of hats and crowns in the booth before choosing a tall crown studded with fake diamonds.

"Gorgeous!" said the photographer, snapping away as Bella came out shyly to stand beside Amber. Louie pretended to be sick in a nearby planter. "It'll look lovely in a gold frame. Frames are an extra five pounds, madam,"

he said sideways to Suzi. "That's it, Princesses!

All done!"

Bella and Amber reluctantly went back into

the booth to take off the lovely princess dresses.

31

"That was brilliant," said Amber. She stroked the yellow satin dress before she put it back on its hanger. "I hope the pictures come out OK."

Pepper put his rough brown nose in through the booth curtain. Bella snatched up Amber's conical hat and balanced it on Pepper's head. He looked adorable, until it slid off sideways.

"You should do pet photos," Amber giggled as they came out of the booth. Two more little girls rushed in, with blue and white dresses over their arms. "Snowy would look so funny in a crown!"

Bella giggled as well. Then suddenly, she stopped. A fantastic idea had sailed into her head.

What if they got some doggie outfits, and did a stand in the Dolphins, and offered photos of people's pets all dressed up? They could do backgrounds, and have all kinds of outfits. Cowboys, fairies, ladybirds...

They'd make a fortune!

"Little dog-bath, here we come!" Bella breathed.

Three

Dressing Up

Suzi was quiet for ages when Bella described her
Big Idea.

"Wouldn't it be expensive?" she said at last.

"It would totally be worth it!" Bella insisted.
"Look how many people did this Princess for a
Day thing!"

"But what about the costumes?" Suzi said helplessly.

"We could make some," Amber suggested.

"I'll help!" offered Claire, listening with interest.

"We could buy them on the Internet," Bella said. She was tumbling over her words. "Or we could ask Mr Chung in Paws 'n' Purrs to order them. It would be brilliant, Mum! You could photograph dogs with their owners, or by themselves. We could have backgrounds and everything."

"You could do footballing outfits for dogs," Louie giggled. "It would be wicked."

"I'm sure it's much too complicated," said Suzi. But she sounded excited as she said it. "Come on, let's quickly pop into Paws 'n' Purrs.

We need some food for Pepper. Then we really have to get back."

Paws 'n' Purrs was Bella's favourite shop. It smelled of sawdust and dog biscuits, and always had exciting things by the counter, like special dog leads and funny balls and squeaky toys. The cages behind the counter were filled with little furry hamsters, gerbils and guinea pigs, and the back of the shop was piled high with animal food. Every now and again, the air would fill with the deafening screech of the large blue and yellow macaw called Adrian, who lived in a large cage by the front door.

"We can order some pet outfits for you,"
nodded the pet shop owner, Mr Chung, when
Bella asked him. "You can dress your dogs up
as anything these days."

"Rar!" squawked Adrian the macaw.

Bella looked around to tell her mum how easy it would be to get hold of the outfits. She saw Louie gazing at a bright yellow corn snake snoozing under a heat lamp, then spotted Suzi at the back of the shop. Bella's mum was lifting a large bag of dog food off a shelf, with the help of a tall man in a bright red tie.

"I use this food for Poppy, my Yorkie," the man was saying. "It's wonderful for her coat."

Bella heard a little yip. She glanced down at her feet. A little Yorkshire terrier was sitting in a basket, a red ribbon tying her long fur off her pretty little face.

"Oh!" Bella gasped. She bent down. "You're lovely!"

The Yorkie yipped again. She had merry little eyes, and a long silky coat that changed colour, from her caramel-brown head to her soft grey back. Tethered outside the shop, Pepper growled.

"Thanks ever so much."

Bella's mum put the big bag of dog food on the counter and smiled at the man with the red tie. The little Yorkie yipped and scrabbled at her basket.

"Is this Poppy?" Suzi asked, looking down.

The man unbuckled the basket and lifted the tiny dog into his arms.

"Yes," he said. "Isn't she pretty?"

Poppy yipped and squirmed in the man's arms.

"My mum runs a dog-grooming

parlour," said Bella at once. Poppy was even smaller and cuter than Crystal. Imagine if Poppy came to Dream Dogs one day!

"This is my marketing manager," said Suzi with a grin. "Otherwise known as my daughter, Bella. Bella, this is Mr Mitchell."

"You run a dog parlour, you say?" said Mr Mitchell. "Wonderful! I've recently moved to Sandmouth and I need a parlour for Poppy. Her coat needs a great deal of attention, as I'm sure you know. Do you do small dogs?"

Suzi hesitated. "We do," she said. "But I'm afraid we don't have any special small-dog equipment."

Mr Mitchell pulled a face. "You don't use a

sink, do you?" he said. "I once tried that for Poppy, and spent hours untangling her fur from the plughole."

Bella glanced at her mum, then looked away again quickly before she giggled.

"Yes," said Suzi with a straight face. "I hear that can happen."

Pepper yapped outside the door. Suzi glanced at her watch and gasped.

"Oh dear, we have to go!" she said. "My next appointment is in ten minutes!"

Bella rolled her eyes. Her mum was always late for *everything*.

Suzi rummaged quickly in her bag and pulled out a Dream Dogs business card. "Come and see us any time!" she called, thrusting the card at Mr Mitchell. Then she paid Mr Chung for the dog food and started running out of the shop.

Bella grabbed Louie and they followed. Bella glanced wistfully back over her shoulder at Poppy, who was still in Mr Mitchell's arms. She hadn't even stroked the little Yorkie. Bella imagined her fur would be as smooth as the pink princess dress.

Oh, she hoped Poppy would come to Dream Dogs – and soon!

Accident!

"Here, Mum," said Bella eagerly. "I'll take those!"

Suzi handed over an armful of doggie outfits in their plastic wrappers. Mr Chung had been as good as his word, and had ordered seven different costumes for the Dream Dogs photo shoot. There was a cowboy, a pirate, a fairy, a

princess, a Chinese emperor, a footballer and a
Robin Hood.

Bella couldn't wait to see the outfits
properly. She rushed up the stairs with Pepper
clattering behind her, and spread them out on
the living-room floor. Some of the outfits were
for big dogs and some were for small. Mr
Chung had thought of everything!

Louie jumped off the sofa and snatched up
the footballing outfit. "Brilliant!" he breathed.
"Can we try it on Pepper?"

"No one can use the outfits until the
weekend," Suzi warned, coming into the living
room.

Bella was disappointed. She would have

loved to see Pepper as a footballer.

"I don't want them getting ripped or spoiled," Suzi said. "Everything's booked at the Dolphins. We just need to print posters and flyers."

"Who's taking the photos?" asked Bella, thinking of the Princess for a Day photographer. The picture of her and Amber was in pride of place beside her bed.

"Me," said Suzi. "I've got a good camera, and it'll save money. We'll set up near that chemist who does instant developing, so we can give the customers their pictures as soon as we can. Goodness, these are cute, aren't they?" she added, picking up the little fairy wings and holding them against herself.

"Imagine Crystal wearing

them! Mimi would love it!"

"What are we going to

do for the backgrounds?"

Louie asked.

"We'll keep it simple," Suzi

told them. "Seven lengths of

different coloured material, all plain. Can I ask

you two to do the posters and flyers?"

"Yeah!" said Louie at once. He loved doing

things on the computer. "Leave it to us, Mum!"

Downstairs, the salon door buzzed.

"That'll be my eleven o'clock," said Suzi.

"You two be good up here."

"We'll start work on the posters," Bella promised.

As soon as Suzi had gone down to the salon, Louie eagerly switched on the computer. "There's this template that Jamie's dad showed me how to do," he said, clicking expertly. "Look! Cool, isn't it?"

They worked together on the computer, typing DREAM DOGS PHOTO SHOOT and DRESS UP YOUR DOG! on the template. It was going to look *great*.

By the time they had finished, just one thing was missing. They needed a photo. Something to show the customers what they would get for their money...

Thoughtfully Bella looked at Pepper, who was now snoozing on the sofa. Then she eyed the doggie outfits still scattered across the floor. Their mum wouldn't mind if they used an outfit to advertise the photo shoot, would she?

Bella made a decision. "Come on, Pepper," she said, reaching for the footballing outfit. "You can be our model."

"Excellent!" Louie cheered.

Bella unwrapped the little blue and white football strip. She carefully lifted Pepper's paws and pushed them through the holes in the blue top, and the holes in the white shorts. Then she pulled his tail out through the tail hole at the back of the shorts.

"There!" she giggled.

Louie fell about laughing. Pepper looked pleased with himself and started racing round the coffee table.

"It's... Idaho Taylor!" Louie choked, holding his tummy. "Heading... for the goal!"

Giggling like a mad thing, Bella dashed out to fetch a foam football from Louie's room. With the ball tucked under her arm, she swerved into the kitchen to pull her mum's camera out of a drawer.

Louie saw the football and fell into fresh gales of laughter.

"Shhh," Bella said, still giggling wildly. "Get Pepper to sit beside the ball... There! Perfect!"

Bella had to stand outside the living-room

door to get the shot. Pepper sat beside the ball,

panting loudly.

"No," said Louie suddenly. "We need an

action shot. I'll kick the ball and Pepper can

dive after it and then you can take the picture!"

Before Bella could stop him, Louie had taken a run at the ball and kicked it hard. The ball sailed out of the living room, smack into Bella.

"Ooof!" said Bella, losing her balance and sitting down very suddenly.

The camera sailed out of Bella's hands, bounced once on the carpet – and fell straight down the stairs behind her.

Bounce, bounce, bounce... *CRACK.*

Five

Big Day Number One

"I'm sorry, Mum," Bella said miserably ten minutes later. "We were trying to do a photo for the poster."

Suzi stared at the sorry state that was her camera. The screen was cracked and the battery had bounced into a corner. She rubbed her forehead with her fingers.

"Oh, Bella," she sighed.

"It was my fault," said Louie.

Suzi shook her head. "It doesn't matter whose fault it was," she said. "Now we need a new camera or a proper photographer who can do our photo shoot this weekend. I've got no *idea* how to find a photographer, and both ideas are expensive. We seem to be getting further away from our plan to get a small dog-bath, not closer."

The salon door tinkled. Everyone looked round. Louie took the opportunity to run back up to the flat and out of trouble's way.

"Hello?" said Mr Mitchell, standing in the

doorway. Poppy peeped out of her basket and barked.

Bella almost forgot how bad she was feeling. Poppy had come to Dream Dogs!

"I don't suppose you can fit me in now, can you?" Mr Mitchell asked hopefully. "I meant to

call, but I've been in such a rush all day."

Bella watched her mum change from a person cross about a broken camera into a person in charge of a dog salon. "Of course I can," Suzi said brightly. "Come in."

Mr Mitchell looked relieved. He put Poppy's basket down on the window seat and flipped up the latch.

"Can I stroke her?" Bella asked shyly.

"I always brush her coat before I wash her," said Mr Mitchell. "You could help me, if you like."

Bella could hardly believe her luck. One minute she was in the biggest trouble of her life. The next minute, she had a dog-brush in her hands and she was carefully combing Poppy the Yorkie's beautiful fur. It felt just the way she had dreamed it would. She let it run through her fingers the way she did when she played with Amber's hair.

Suzi lifted Poppy into the big bath and turned the shower attachment to a weak flow. Bella rested her head on the edge of the bath and watched as Suzi bent awkwardly over the bath and started wetting the Yorkie's fur. The little dog looked a bit lonely in the bathtub. It was like staring at a pea on a big white plate.

"So what brings you to Sandmouth, Mr Mitchell?" Suzi asked, working the shampoo into a lather on Poppy's back.

"Call me George," said Mr Mitchell. "I needed more space for my work than I had in London, and the light in Sandmouth is wonderful. So I moved here. I'm a photographer, you see."

Bella's chin almost slipped off the edge of the bath. A *photographer*?

"Goodness," Suzi gasped. "I don't suppose you're free to do a job this weekend, are you?"

Mr Mitchell pulled a diary out of his top pocket and checked it. "Yes," he said, closing the pages. "I am. What did you have in mind?"

On Saturday morning, Bella stood in the Dolphins shopping centre with Amber. They both clutched flyers in their hands. People were walking past them, up and down and up and down. Pepper stood beside Amber, barking merrily. He was wearing the cowboy hat on his head.

"Photograph your dog today!" Amber shouted, waving a flyer over her head and trying to get people's attention. "Great choice of costumes! Only four pounds ninety-nine!"

"By Filbert's Pharmacy!" Bella joined in. "Dream Dogs Photos while you wait!" Whenever she saw someone go past with a dog, she made her voice extra loud. "Pet photos! They make brilliant gifts!"

"Let's go and see how your mum and Mr Mitchell are getting on," Amber suggested after a while. "We've been giving out flyers for ages. They must have some customers by now."

Bella stuffed the remaining flyers into her bag and ran with Amber down the mall. Even

though she had helped to set up the
photography stand earlier that morning, Bella
couldn't help feeling a skip of excitement when
she saw it standing outside Filbert's Pharmacy.
They didn't need the developing machine at the
pharmacy because Mr Mitchell had brought his
own computer and printer. But it was still a
great spot. There was a platform for the dogs
to stand on, and a big background screen
draped in the long red cloth and topped with
the Dream Dogs logo. The doggie outfits hung
on a rail. Everything was ready. But apart from
her mum, Mr Mitchell, Louie, Claire and
Amber's dog, Snowy, there was nobody near
the stall.

"Where are all the customers?" Bella asked.

"I don't know," Suzi sighed. "Maybe we didn't advertise it properly."

"But we've given out loads of flyers!" said Amber in dismay.

"How many people had their dogs with them?" Suzi asked.

Bella thought. "Maybe three," she said.

From her basket, Poppy gave a little yip. Bella went over and made a fuss of the little dog through the basket window. She was wearing a yellow ribbon in her fur today.

"I'm very sorry, George," said Suzi, turning to Mr Mitchell. She sounded close to tears. "What a waste of a day for you."

"Don't worry about me," said Mr Mitchell. "I wasn't doing anything else today. Besides, they might still come."

Everyone waited. Getting bored, Louie jumped up and down on the platform and pulled silly faces.

"Get off, Louie!" Bella said crossly. "You'll break it!"

"Tell you what, Suzi," said Claire, after a hopeless forty minutes. "Why don't we dress up Snowy, just to start the ball rolling?"

Snowy was a big black spaniel. Amber had called him Snowy as a joke, and the name had stuck. Bella helped Amber to dress Snowy up as Robin Hood. Strapping the little quiver of pretend arrows on to Snowy's back, Bella felt more cheerful.

"Let's have a green backcloth," Claire suggested. "Sherwood Forest and all that!"

Suzi arranged the green cloth. Amber put the Robin Hood hat on Snowy's head and adjusted the elastic under his chin. Snowy sat

patiently, wagging his tail every now and then.

One or two people began to gather around the

stand to watch.

"Perfect," said Mr Mitchell in an encouraging

voice. "Now, Snowy, up on the platform!"

Snowy took a flying leap on to the platform.

Dream Dogs

There was a terrible CRASH as the platform collapsed. The big spaniel yelped and took off down the mall. With a wobble, the backscreen tipped over. Then the clothes rail fell over with a clang, scattering the costumes and the big green blackcloth billowed gently to the ground, covering Louie from head to foot.

Six

Big Day Number Two

Over breakfast on Tuesday morning, Suzi pushed aside the new edition of the *Sandmouth Bugle* with a sigh. The headline on page three read "DOGGIE DISASTER!" A big photograph of Louie and Pepper and the big green cloth took up the rest of the front page. The Dream Dogs sign lay on the ground at Louie's feet.

Louie giggled into his cereal.

"I don't know what you're laughing about, Louie," said Suzi. "This is all very embarrassing."

"I *said* you shouldn't jump on that platform," Bella told her little brother. "Didn't I?"

"It wasn't me," Louie protested. "It was *Snowy*, in case you didn't notice."

"Yes, but you must have broken it earlier when you jumped on it," Bella snapped, "so when Snowy—"

The phone rang.

"Hello?" said Suzi. "Yes, this is Dream Dogs... Yes— a dog parlour, that's right... Did you find

us in the telephone directory? Ah. Yes, well,
that was a bit of a disaster. I— What did you
say?"

Bella watched as her mum scribbled
something down on the pad of paper that lived
by the phone. When she hung up, Suzi had a
funny look on her face.

"Who was that?" Bella asked.

"Someone wanting to book their dog in for a
photograph next weekend," said Suzi slowly.
"They saw us in the paper."

"It's a shame they're too late," said Louie.

The phone rang again.

"Hello?" said Suzi.

It was another enquiry about photographs.

69

Three more followed before Bella had finished her toast. Maybe their Big Disaster hadn't been such a disaster after all.

Suzi looked dazed as the phone went for the sixth time. "Hello, Dream Dogs?" She looked helplessly at Bella.

"Tell them you'll do it again next weekend!" said Bella, forming a plan in her mind. "It's perfect, Mum!"

"But we don't know if Mr Mitchell can do it!" said Suzi, hanging up. "Oh bother, the phone's going again. Hello, Dream Dogs...?"

Bella rushed down the stairs to the salon.

She found Mr Mitchell's number and dialled it.

He answered straight away.

"Can you do the photographs again next
weekend instead, Mr Mitchell?" Bella asked
breathlessly. "We're getting loads of requests
from people who've seen us in the paper!"

"Of course," said Mr Mitchell promptly. In
the background, Bella could hear Poppy
woofing.

She took the stairs back up to the flat two at
a time. Pepper watched curiously from his
basket in the kitchen as Bella told her mum and
Louie the good news.

"Goodness," said Suzi. She started to laugh
as the phone rang again. "There's nothing like

free advertising, is there? Next weekend it is!"

"Look at all the dogs!" Bella gasped.

It was the following Saturday, and they were back in the Dolphins. Everywhere Bella looked, there were dogs on leads. The shopping centre echoed with barks and yaps. There was no need for flyers today.

"Form a queue!" Claire called, as people jostled around the Dream Dogs photography stand. "Please, we can only do one of you at a time!"

"Wow," Amber breathed. "I feel like I'm at a dog show or something."

Mr Chung came out of Paws 'n' Purrs, carrying a large bag of dog food for a customer with two Shelties. He waved cheerfully at Bella. It looked as if the Dream Dogs photo disaster had brought plenty of business for him as well. Bella was glad.

"Oh, look," Amber breathed. "Mr Mitchell is doing one of Poppy!"

The little Yorkie sat on the platform with her head on one side. A set of sparkly fairy wings were on her back and a chiffon skirt was wrapped around her waist. She looked adorable against the pale pink blackcloth.

"I want that picture," Bella giggled. "Do you think Mr Mitchell will let me have it?"

73

The stand was doing very good business. Suzi

and Claire helped the customers to get their

dogs to get dressed in the different outfits.

Louie was changing the backcloth to whatever

colour the customer liked. He climbed up and

down the stepladder, hanging the different

colours and even suggesting colours to

customers who weren't sure.

Mr Mitchell changed cameras. He handed his first camera to Bella.

"Do you know how to plug this into the computer?" he asked.

Bella nodded. She'd done it lots of times with her mum's old camera.

"Good," said Mr Mitchell. "You can start printing the pictures, Bella. They're all numbered, and the numbers match this sheet here so we don't get muddled. Check them before you print them, won't you? Pick a single shot of each dog."

Taking the camera, Bella plugged it into the computer with a long black wire. The pictures appeared on the computer screen. Bella carefully went through them. Mr Mitchell had done a brilliant job. The dogs all looked so cute! She skipped over one or two pictures which showed people in the background, or where the dogs were blurred or not looking properly at the camera. Then she pressed the print button. As if by magic, photos began to pour out.

Bella scooped up an armful of pictures and started sorting them, checking their numbers and putting them into envelopes for the customers.

"Oh!" she gasped as she suddenly lost her grip on a handful of photographs. They

cascaded to the floor in a heap. For a horrible

moment, Bella thought she'd never be able to

sort them out. Then she remembered Mr

Mitchell's system. She just had to match the

numbers on the screen to the photos and

everything would be fine.

A lady in a smart red suit bent down to help

her pick the pictures up again.

"Thanks," said Bella breathlessly.

"No problem," said the lady with a smile.

She paused at the picture of Poppy. "What a gorgeous shot," she said with interest.

"I know," Bella agreed happily. She took the picture of Poppy and put it in an envelope with MITCHELL written on the front. "I want it in my bedroom!"

Amber helped Bella to fill the rest of the envelopes. Then they handed them over to Suzi, who put them neatly into a filed box, ready for collection.

"Everything all right, love?" said Suzi, pushing her hair out of her eyes.

Bella grinned. "Everything's brilliant," she said.

The Dream Dogs photo shoot stand was busy all day. By four o'clock, the order book was full of names and addresses. Most people returned to collect their pictures before going back to their cars. The rest would go in the post in the morning.

"I've got lots of new business from this," Suzi said happily. She gathered Bella in for a big kiss. "You're a superstar for thinking of it, Bella."

Louie sat at the bottom of the stepladder with his nose buried in a comic as Mr Mitchell put his camera back into its case.

"A good day's work," he said, and smiled at Suzi. "Now all we have to do is cash up!"

Bella had been looking forward to doing this all day. They *must* have made enough money for a little dog-bath. She looked around for the cash box, but couldn't see it.

"Mum?" she called. "Where did you put the cash box?"

"Right there," Suzi began, pointing. Then she gasped.

"The cash box," she whispered in horror. "It's not there!"

Seven

Proof

It was true. The cash box had disappeared.

"Who saw it last?" Bella said in dismay.

"Me," said Suzi, holding her hand to her forehead. "I took ten pounds from the lady with two Dalmatians. It was right *here*. I swear it was!"

But it wasn't. Not any more.

"It looks like someone has taken it," said Mr Mitchell in a grim voice.

Bella's stomach squeezed until it hurt. They had been so busy. It would have been easy for someone to lift the cash box quickly off the table and disappear into the crowds. Bella looked around the Dolphins shopping centre like she'd never seen it before. It was a horrible feeling, knowing that someone out there had taken their money.

"I don't want to come back here, ever," said Louie in a small voice.

Suzi was on the verge of tears. Claire looked upset, and put her arm round Suzi. Bella felt

Amber squeezing her hand. On her other side, Pepper nuzzled her leg comfortingly. Bella gulped. She felt *awful*.

"Is there a problem here?"

A tall, thin policeman was standing by the rail of dog outfits.

"Yes," said Mr Mitchell at once. "We've had a robbery!"

Bella sat down on the platform and tightly held her mum's hand as Mr Mitchell explained what had happened.

"Hmm," said the police officer several times. "All cash, was it?"

"Most of it," said Suzi miserably. "That means we'll never get it back, doesn't it?"

"Did you see the thief?" the police officer asked.

Everyone shook their heads.

"Without a description," the officer began, "we may have trouble finding—" He broke off as his phone rang. "Yes?" he said briskly. "What? Where? I'll be right there…"

The officer slid his phone into his belt. "Does the name Billy Watts mean anything to you?" he asked.

Bella shook her head. Everyone else looked blank.

"Billy Watts has been in trouble for stealing before,"

said the policeman. "I've just had a call from
one of the shopkeepers at the top end of the
mall, saying Billy's been in with a suspicious
amount of money today."

Bella's spirits lifted. "Is he the thief?" she said
eagerly.

"Can we get our money back?" Louie asked.

"Do you remember seeing a man with short
red hair hanging around the stand?" asked the
policeman. "There's a tattoo on his neck, of a
spider's web."

Everyone shook their heads.

The policeman sighed. "Unless someone saw
him near your stand, we can't prove that he
took the money from you," he said. "We'll

arrest him on suspicion of theft. If one of you

can come down to the station and identify him,

we might get somewhere. Otherwise, it's a

hopeless case."

"I can't believe we still have to send out the

rest of these pictures," Louie moaned, back at

the salon two hours later.

Bella and Louie had returned to Dream Dogs

with Mr Mitchell, Claire and Amber. Suzi had

gone down to the police station, to see if she

could identify Billy Watts. Now they were all

waiting for Suzi to come home. Bella hoped

that her mum would recognise Billy Watts. But

she wasn't very hopeful.

"These customers paid us," Mr Mitchell explained to Louie. He scratched Poppy's head as the little Yorkie panted quietly on his lap. "They should get their pictures."

Bella clicked on an image of a chocolate-coloured Labrador wearing the Chinese emperor outfit. Normally it would have made her laugh. Now she barely looked at it. She just concentrated on printing it out. She could feel Pepper sitting on her feet underneath the table. Snowy was lying full-stretch on the sofa, snoring softly.

Claire checked her watch. "I wonder how much longer your mum is going to be?" she said

fretfully. "I need to fetch Joe from his piano lesson."

Bella clicked on the next doggie picture, ready to print it out.

"No good," said Mr Mitchell, looking over her shoulder. "There's someone in the background. Skip past and on to the next one, Bella."

Bella looked closer. Everyone jumped as she leaped out of her chair and pointed at the screen.

"Look!" Bella gasped. "Behind the screen, there! Look at the person!"

Everyone rushed around the computer screen.

"Make it bigger," said Mr Mitchell in excitement.

Bella had already clicked on the zoom button. The picture jumped out of the screen at them. It showed a young man with short red hair walking past the table. The table with the cash box on it.

"Too blurred," said Claire with frustration. "Is there another one?"

Bella rushed to the next shot. Again, the man with red hair. This picture was better. Bella saw something blue on the man's neck. A tattoo?

More importantly, the picture showed the table again.

Only this time, the cash box was nowhere to be seen.

"Now you see it," said Mr Mitchell in amazement as Bella clicked back and forth on the two photographs. Poppy barked and jumped around on his lap. "Now you don't. Bella, you've got him and we've got the proof right here!"

"We have to ring the police station," said Bella. She felt breathless. "We can email the pictures!"

The phone rang. Pepper barked madly as everyone jumped towards it. Even Snowy woke up.

"Mum!" Louie shouted, snatching up the receiver. "We've found the thief! We've got him!"

Bella took the receiver from Louie. She pressed the speakerphone button so everyone could hear.

"Mum, what's the email address at the station?" she said.

Suzi sounded exhausted. "I didn't recognise that man, Billy Watts," she said. "So they're about to let him go."

"NO!" everyone shouted. Pepper barked even more loudly, and started zooming round the coffee table.

"Tell them to keep him there for a bit

longer!" Bella begged.

"Why?" Suzi sounded bewildered. "What was Louie saying? And why do you need an email address?"

"We've got photos, Suzi!" Claire yelled across the room.

"Proof!" Louie sang. "PROOF!"

"Tell the police station to check their email," said Bella as Mr Mitchell went into his email account and attached the two pictures. "Any minute... NOW!"

Eight

Fame at Last

When Suzi came home an hour later, she was carrying two big carrier bags. The salty smell of fish and chips wafted around her.

"Mmm!" said Louie happily as Bella helped her mum carry the bags upstairs. They were warm in her arms.

"Thanks, Suzi," said Claire gratefully.

"Teamwork deserves reward," said Suzi.
"Fish and chips for everyone!"

"Did they arrest him then?" Bella asked
eagerly as everyone settled down around the
kitchen table. Poppy
sniffed at the
vinegar on the
chips and gave a
tiny, delicate
sneeze.

"As soon as they got those pictures, they
certainly did," Suzi said.

"What about the money?" Claire asked.

Suzi fetched the ketchup out of the fridge.

"I'm afraid most of it's gone," she said. "We got what was left, at least."

"How much was that?" Amber asked.

Bella crossed her fingers. Maybe Billy Watts hadn't spent too much. Maybe—

"Eleven pounds fifty," said Suzi.

Bella had known it would be bad. But this was worse than bad. This was *terrible*.

"We'll never get a dog-bath now!" she wailed. Eleven pounds fifty would hardly buy them a washing-up bowl.

"How much do you think we made?" said Claire sadly.

"About three hundred pounds," said George Mitchell.

95

Everyone silently ate their fish. Pepper stole one of Bella's chips and yelped when it burned his tongue.

"Hard luck, Pepper," Bella said miserably. "Life is unfair, isn't it?"

"Well!" said Suzi on Monday morning. "Five appointments today, and three of them new clients. At least Saturday wasn't a *complete* waste of time. I collected *lots* of names and addresses. We'll be able to afford that dog-bath in no time!"

Bella knew her mum was trying to cheer her up. It wasn't working. She unloaded the tumble dryer and began folding up towels.

"George and Poppy are coming at any moment," Suzi went on. "Poppy always cheers you up, Bella!"

But even the thought of Poppy couldn't make Bella smile today. She couldn't forget about all the money that Billy Watts had stolen. She kept thinking of how hard they'd all worked to earn that money. Three hundred pounds wasn't enough to buy a dog-bath, but it was enough to buy a *third* of a dog-bath. And now it was gone. Bella stacked the towels so hard that they fell over in a muffled heap and she had to start again.

"Morning!" said George Mitchell, coming

through with a tinkle of the door. Poppy gazed out of her basket with her bright button eyes.

"Hello, George," Suzi sighed. "Maybe you can cheer up Bella today. I can't do it."

"I don't *want* to cheer up," said Bella fiercely.

She stacked the last towel on top of the pile and stomped out of the salon and up the stairs. When she reached her room she flung herself grumpily on her bed and stared at her pillow.

She heard her bedroom door creak open.

"In the films the goodies always win," said Louie crossly.

"This isn't a film," Bella sighed.

Louie came to sit on Bella's bed. Trotting in behind him came Pepper. Bella glanced at the new photo by her bedside. It showed Pepper in

the football strip, posing beautifully under the

Dream Dogs logo at the Dolphins shopping

centre. She put the picture face-down on her

bedside table. Then she gazed out of the

window.

Bella had a view down to the street from her

bedroom. She frowned when she saw a lady

walking down the road with a briefcase. She recognised the lady from somewhere. But where?

"That lady was at the shopping centre on Saturday," said Louie.

It came to Bella in a flash. It was the lady who had helped to pick up the photographs when Bella had dropped them on the floor.

Curiously, Bella watched as the lady stopped at Dream Dogs. She heard the bell tinkle.

"Something's happening, Louie," she said. She got slowly off her bed. "I can feel it."

"Huh," said Louie.

"Woof," said Pepper.

Louie and Pepper followed Bella down the

stairs. Bella pushed open the door from the hallway to the salon.

"Miranda Hicks, Creative Creatures," the lady was saying as she handed a business card to Suzi and another one to Mr Mitchell.

"You helped me in the shopping centre," said Bella.

Miranda Hicks smiled. "I did," she said. "And that's when I saw a photograph that I want to use. The picture of this gentleman's little Yorkie, dressed as a fairy."

"Her name is Poppy," said Mr Mitchell.

Standing on the drying table, Poppy gave a tiny woof.

"Hello, Poppy," said Miranda Hicks. She

stroked the Yorkie's soft head. "I run an advertising company," she went on. "We use animals in all our advertisements and Poppy would be the perfect model for a big campaign we have coming up. Would you be interested in selling me the rights to that picture?"

"How much?" said Louie, coming out from behind Bella.

"Louie!" Suzi and Bella both scolded at the same time.

"Well, how about two thousand pounds, Mr Mitchell?" said Miranda.

Bella sat down suddenly on the window seat. Louie started jumping around like he had springs on his feet.

"George, that's brilliant!" Suzi exclaimed.

Mr Mitchell looked stunned. "Two thousand pounds?" he said. "Of course I'll accept! But only if you'll take half, Suzi."

Now it was Suzi's turn to sit down. "You don't mean it, George," she gasped.

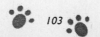

"Yes, I do," said George Mitchell firmly. "It was your photo shoot, and your costume. Take half for Dream Dogs, Suzi. Please."

"Dog-bath!" Bella sang. "Dog-bath, dog-bath, dog-bath!"

"Thank you, George," said Suzi. Her voice was a bit wobbly. "If you're absolutely sure, then I will."

A month later, a little dog-bath stood at the back of the Dream Dogs salon. It went silently up and down at the press of a button. There was a special door set in the side of the bath, and a ramp.

"You can stop pressing that button now, Louie," Suzi laughed.

Louie put the remote control down reluctantly as the bath sank to the ground for the third time. A red ribbon was tied across the open doorway.

"I declare this dog-bath open," Bella announced in her loudest voice.

Pepper barked as she snipped the ribbon through with a pair of her mum's grooming scissors. Everyone cheered. Lots of their friends were in the salon today, including George Mitchell and the guest of honour, Poppy. Miss Waldicott and Angus were there, with Mimi and Crystal and Mr Evans with his two golden

Dream Dogs

retrievers, Barney and Nugget. Also in the parlour were Mrs Frost and Charlie the Labradoodle, Mr Flynn with his German shepherd, Alfie, Sophie Olowu and her mum with their two puppies, Buttercup and Sandy, and Amber and Claire with Snowy, of course.

"The first customer, please!" said Suzi.

Poppy gave a little bark. She sniffed the door, and trotted up the ramp and into the bath. Louie pressed a button. The door slid shut and the little bath rose silently upwards.

"Before you start washing Poppy, Suzi," said George Mitchell, "I've got something to put on the Dream Dogs pinboard."

He pulled a folder out of his bag, and carefully removed something. It was the photograph of Poppy dressed as a fairy, cut from the page of a large glossy magazine. Underneath the picture was a set of pink dog-grooming products. Bella read the caption and giggled.

FOR HAIRY FAIRIES EVERYWHERE.

"To Dream Dogs!" somebody cried, as glasses clinked together. "The best dog parlour in the world!"

Top tips from vets!

Although it can seem cute or funny to dress dogs up in outfits, they are happiest when they are behaving naturally – like dogs should! We've got some great tips on how to get your dog looking and smelling fab without the need for costumes.

 It's great to give your dog a bath from time to time, but remember when you bathe them it can remove natural oils which keep the skin healthy, so use a special doggie shampoo and coat conditioner.

 Dogs, especially puppies, can get cold very easily, so bath them in a draught-free area and dry them straight away with a warm, fluffy towel that's their very own. Allow your dog to get used to being bathed by giving them treats and praise – first for being in the bath, then when the water is running, then when they let you put some water on them.

 Keep 'bathtime' calm and relaxed, or else your dog may get stressed and you will get drenched!

 Remember that dogs benefit from protection from cold and rain, just as we do. A sensible doggie raincoat and warm fleece if they need it will keep your dog warm and snug when you go out for a walk.

Could your pet be famous? Check out our online gallery of cute pets at www.pdsa.org.uk/petprotectors and send in a picture of your pet too!

pdsa

for pets in need of vets

Help PDSA by joining our Pet Protectors Club!

PDSA treats the sick and injured pets of people in need.

For kids who love pets

Members get ...

Membership badge and card

Cute stickers

Animal year planner

Plus a free bag!

Animal Antics

Just £11 a year!

Personalised fridge magnet

magazine every 2 months

Sign me up!

Fill in the form and send it with a cheque or postal order for £11 made payable to 'PDSA' to PDSA Pet Protectors, Whitechapel Way, Priorslee, Telford, Shropshire TF2 9PQ.

Name .... Date of birth ....

Address ....

....

Postcode ....

Telephone ....

Protecting your information Leading veterinary charity, PDSA, uses your information to manage your membership of Pet Protectors; we will never pass these details on to anyone else for marketing purposes. Occasionally we may like to send you details of local PDSA events and activities. If you do not want us to do this, please tick this box. ☐

Registered charity nos. 208217 & SC037585

for pets in need of vets

DD_Pepper_2010

Join online www.youngpdsa.org.uk or join by phone on 0800 019 9144

Take home all of the
Dream Dogs

If you have it, tick it!